STERLING CHILDREN'S BOOKS
New York

An Imprint of Sterling Publishing
387 Park Avenue South
New York, NY 10016

Text © 2015 by Marjorie Blain Parker
Illustrations © 2015 by Jed Henry
The illustrations were created using pencil, pastels, and digital brushes.
Designed by Andrea Miller

ISBN 978-1-4549-0507-3

Library of Congress Cataloging-in-Publication Data

Parker, Marjorie Blain.
I love you near and far / by Marjorie Blain Parker ; illustrated by Jed Henry.
  pages cm
Summary: Rhyming text relates how a child deals with missing Dad and Grandma, who both live far away.
ISBN 978-1-4549-0507-3
[1. Stories in rhyme. 2. Separation (Psychology)--Fiction. 3. Love--Fiction. 4. Parent and child--Fiction. 5. Grandparent and child--Fiction.] I. Henry, Jed, illustrator. II. Title.

PZ8.3.P1695Iam 2015
[E]--dc23

2013047210

Distributed in Canada by Sterling Publishing
c/o Canadian Manda Group, 165 Dufferin Street
Toronto, Ontario, Canada M6K 3H6
Distributed in the United Kingdom by GMC Distribution Services
Castle Place, 166 High Street, Lewes, East Sussex, England BN7 1XU
Distributed in Australia by Capricorn Link (Australia) Pty. Ltd.
P.O. Box 704, Windsor, NSW 2756, Australia

For information about custom editions, special sales, and premium and corporate purchases, please contact
Sterling Special Sales at 800-805-5489 or specialsales@sterlingpublishing.com.

Manufactured in China
Lot #:
2 4 6 8 10 9 7 5 3 1
05/14

www.sterlingpublishing.com/kids

I Love You Near and Far

by Marjorie Blain Parker • illustrated by Jed Henry

STERLING CHILDREN'S BOOKS
New York

I know that we live far away,
far apart.

But I can still **love you**
with all of my heart.

I love all your letters
and air-mailed treasure.

I love you long distance,
like no map can measure.

I love you with pictures
and bright online smiles.

I love you wherever,
across all those miles.

Wherever you live—
if it's near or it's far . . .

I love you wherever,
wherever you are.

I love you with phone calls—
there's so much to say.

I love you wherever,
though we're hours away.

I love you completely—
from bottom to top.

I love you wherever.
I love you **nonstop**.

Wherever you live—
if it's near or it's far . . .

I love you wherever,
wherever you are.

But, sometimes, it just gets
too hard to miss you.

And I must find a way
to hold, hug, and kiss you!

So jump in a car,

and then hop on a train,

so I can love you in person—
days of laughing and caring,

making memories together
for saving and sharing.

So, wherever you live—
if it's near or it's far . . .

I will love you wherever,
Wherever you are.